TEXTBOOK FOLLIES

A NOVEL

Cory J. Schulman

Textbook Follies

Cory J. Schulman

Germantown, Maryland

Best Seller Publications, LLC

ISBN: 978-0-9962344-6-7

Library of Congress Control Number: 1-11160481771

BISAC: FIC019000

BestSellerPublications.com

BestSellerPublications@gmail.com

Also by Cory J. Schulman:

The Writer's Story

When Time Was Endless

The World of Comics

A Postcard from Jerusalem

Other books published by BSP:

Dual Mission

Ex-Cops and Robbers

Living With Madness

Messages to the author or publisher may be sent to
BestSellerPublications@gmail.com

Table of Contents

1　The Beginning of the Rest of My Life

The celebratory mood at a college graduation party contrasted my moment of depression. I reluctantly attended, because who wouldn't want to acknowledge the academic accomplishment of completing a four-year degree? At least statistically, I was part of the "educated" class, the upper echelon poised to move the earth and shake up society, ablaze with ambition, unmovable integrity, and an unstoppable pursuit of a better world!

After the photos of me and my friends garbed in black robes and tasseled flat, square hats, Sharone, a friend of the graduating class, invited me to the post-graduation party at her family's home near the college. Sharone was a local student, who lived with her parents in a well-to-do part of town. The family home boasted a back-yard swimming pool, which served as a perfect environment to host a barbecue for a group of six closely-knit graduates.

Our friendships developed as the semesters came and went. We became associated with friends of friends until the group of associates grew amongst the class of 1986. The six of us lived together in an off-campus house during our senior year. We learned about each other's passions through our declared majors and watched each other struggle to adhere to disciplined study of thick textbooks.

We understood the mental anguish from anxiety-driven nights readying for accumulative tests and painstakingly writing 20-page research papers. We all witnessed the metamorphoses of our belief systems as freshman be challenged until we acquired not only the fundamentals of knowledge, but more importantly an understanding of cognitive approaches, analytical skills, ability to question, research, and above all, differentiate the folly from the reality, as best one could.

The dorm-room bull sessions, the philosophical debates, and the politics of the day intrigued us all with lively, if not raucous discourse. Our socio-economic, religious, and ethnic persuasions intermingled with our personality traits, local customs, and variances of maturity. We were a melting pot of diverse backgrounds and behaviors. In the end we made personal decisions to party, indulge in alcohol and drug use, and experiment with sex. Who slept with whom? How often with how many different partners. We were all just trying to figure out our own tolerances, pleasures, and principles while affronted with judgments from our peers, who whether friend or detractor, still became part of the group that experienced college together and who would become an indelible part of our collective memories.

Despite the smiles and excitement at the barbecue, I sat off to the side with my head collapsed on my arms, which held my knees tightly.

Sharone approached me, noticing my dejected mood. "Hey, Roy, this is supposed to be a happy time. What's going on?"

I smiled back at Sharone and simply said, "It's the end of an era."

She shot back, "And the beginning of the rest of our lives. Cheer up."

I stewed about the end and loss of the world I've known for the past four years. Despite the brutality of self-doubt, the periodic failings of submitting this or that paper on time, and the discouraging grades which were compounded by anxiety, depression, burnout, and lack of love, I knew my life, while bittersweet, was a known quantity. And just as I was finally feeling at ease, it ended.

No longer would I be surrounded by thousands of young, healthy cohorts. No longer would I wake up and stroll across campus to my classes and receive a clear, organized lecture on the depths of an abstruse subject. No longer would I live expense free or simply go to the cafeteria to eat. My mentally challenging, but structured life would suddenly now be gone.

The passage of academia is supposed to be a good thing. For now, the future is open with all possibilities. I can do and go anywhere and earn a good living. That was the expectation of the graduate. Yet, after about 30 different classes and three changes of my major over the past four years, I still didn't know what I wanted to do with my life. The future was blank with the unknown. And fear consumed me.

***

The next day, I parted with the campus and returned with my carload of belongings to Gaithersburg, Maryland to my family's home. The sudden resumption of life under the governance of parents seemed almost a cruel sense of time travel into the past where I was subjected to house rule, lack of privacy, and subservience within a hierarchical kingdom. Was my education a lie? Did I not grow and become a man? At 6:00 pm, my mother called out from a floor below, "Roy…Dinner's ready." Like a Pavlovian research animal, my mouth salivated at the sound of my mother's announcement.

Instead of intense philosophical exchanges and banter amongst friends, I listened to dinner conversation that peaked intensity with an acknowledgement that the steak was well marbled. Questions of Plato and Socrates never entered the discussion. There wasn't even a coherent discussion, just silence interrupted with the occasional commentary on the savings we realized when shopping at Magruder's and using the coupons clipped from *The Washington Post*. The difference in intensity and passion from the college setting to the family seemed to remake the world into a slow-motion caricature. Sitting at the table, I felt as if I needed to scream.

Why isn't anyone talking about where the beef was processed and whether the slaughterhouse was sanitary and humane, and what was the statistical risk of getting a food-borne illness? Did my parents know how much more resources it took to feed a cow before it got slaughtered than to eat a vegetarian meal? But I just sat pacified in a near stupor of resignation. I felt as if I were an extra in a play whose role was to exist among the periphery as an anonymous being who had no lines and shouldn't distract from the main show.

I was not the dominant leader in this primate clan. I was subservient to persons who I perceived as stuck in the 1940s. My father finally said something different from coupon savings and how good the meat was. But it was, even if inadvertent, derisive, "Roy, when are you getting a haircut?" My hair was lush, thick, jet black with shoulder length, gentle curls and bangs that reached my brows. My hair was symbolic of youth, vigor, and of the 1980s. But to my father who came of age in the 1940s, I looked like I wore a mop on my head. His very question perturbed me. No questions about how I felt or any suggestions what to do about a job. Just my appearance, which not only was by design, but in a way just as shallow a subject as the rarity of the meat. I resented the topic altogether. Yet he continued, but only to belabor the point, "You know you'll need a haircut to go on interviews. You can't show up like that." He said, as if I were horribly disfigured by my own hand.

The days after graduation turned into weeks. With each passing day, I worried more and more about the question: *What was I going to do with my life?* After changing my major three times and reading the entirety of about 75 different textbooks, you would think I would at least know what I wanted to do. But I had been a humanities student, majoring in psychology, which required graduate school to qualify for a professional position. After four years of college, I was burned out from studying. I didn't want to return to school. I knew that much. So, I had a degree that didn't open any doors for me. If I pursued the opportunities that a psychology degree offered, I would end up teaching mentally disabled adults daily living skills, such as bathing, dressing, and eating. I would be changing soiled underpants, and trying to discipline persons who at times behaved out of control. Not that this role is unimportant. But I just knew I saw myself in a more professional, white-collar job. Likewise, I couldn't see myself in graduate school studying textbooks for another second. I was ready to work in the real world.

I scoured the newspaper for classified ads, however, all of the job openings required not only a degree but also a minimum of three to five years of experience. The Catch-22 concept was quickly instilled in me. How could I get my first career job, if they all required having had a first job? Didn't my degree qualify me? To that I knew the answer, "no." No employer wanted a recent graduate unless their degree was from a prestigious school, which my state college was not.

The way some graduates handled the Catch-22 situation was to work in an internship even before graduation so that they could indicate relevant experience right after receiving their degree. I neither had such foresight, nor the academic will to take on such extra responsibility in conjunction with my full-time coursework. Hence here I existed, living at my family's home having my dinner cooked for me and looking like a human sheep head.

***

Dealing day after day with no agenda felt deflating. I scoured the classifieds each day, but within ten minutes I concluded that there were no realistic opportunities for me. After ten minutes of discipline each day, the rest of the day remained available for consumption.

I occupied my time in a way that came naturally. I picked up my basketball and headed for the local park to shoot hoops and hope to participate in a pickup game with other stray players.

I engaged in set shots, layups, turnaround jump shots. All the while, my imagination transported me in the middle of a competitive game, five against five, full court, a referee, and bleachers full of cheering spectators. My mind's eye captured the unfolding drama, the quick passes and drives into the middle of the lane toward the basket, dribbling inches from the hardwood, circling opponents and leaping up in parallel with the defender only to fake a shot, retract the ball then double pump with a poised, intentional toss of the ball that rolled off my fingertips and seemingly floated above the rim to fall into the hoop as effortlessly as were my days living at home.

"The crowd goes wild," as I retrieved the ball and realized the reality that I played alone in an otherwise unoccupied park. I continued playing until dusk when the rim was harder to see against the darkening sky. I walked home on tender feet which developed blisters from all the pivoting and jerking of my body to fake out imaginary opponents.

Upon entry into my family's home, I smelled the aroma of the evening meal. I deposited my ball in the coat closet and dashed upstairs to shower and change. When I entered the kitchen, my family was already seated at a table set and ready for dinner. My father greeted me, "Well look who shows up at the right time, 'living the life of Riley.'" He was trying to be jovial, but somehow it panged me as an overly critical remark that suggested I was a leach living the good life without responsibility. Inwardly, I could see that's exactly the situation I was in, but by default. I didn't design it this way. I was just in this nowhere spot now, supposedly temporarily until I secured a real job. Then I could move out and live my life independently with privacy and peace away from disparaging remarks, even if inadvertent.

The days of basketball, lying in bed listening to my stereo albums, and simply ruminating about a job made the days all seem indistinguishable from each other; each day became "blursday." But for the first time in many years, I felt well rested. I no longer crammed for tests and wrote research papers all night long without sleep. The constant anxieties resulting from poor time management skills, finally was sleighed with the end of college. But now I faced faceless days of ennui. I slept long hours then lounged, and watched television.

As weeks passed, I continued preoccupying my days with passivity interrupted by outings with my basketball. As a change of pace, one Saturday, I took my tennis racket and walked to the tennis courts of my former high school. Several other people, some couples, some individuals, were running about in bee-like irregular movements on the courts chasing balls and whacking returns to their opponents. Starting and stopping, moving forward then back, then to side, pivoting and reaching, swinging and swatting the tennis ball back to its origination.

No one was without a partner, so I was resigned to watch the various levels of talent before me. As I entertained myself watching, I heard my name called out from behind me. I turned and recognized Rick Michaels, a high school alum who was my wrestling partner at that time. "Michaels," I said surprised, immediately recognizing his solid build and red hair after a four-year hiatus.

"Come to get beat at tennis, Roy?" he said with a competitive edge.

"A court on the far side just opened," I replied pointing my racket to the available court.

We headed to the court with little exchange of small talk nor a nostalgic revisit to our shared time in high school. Only a brief update. Michaels was reticent. I had to pry open any information by pelting him with questions. His replies were always curt. I asked him what he's been doing since high school. He simply said, "Engineering school, you?"

I obliged him, "I just graduated from State College, but with a degree in psychology. I can't do much with just a B.A. degree in the field. Unless I want to teach severely psychologically impaired patients how to properly use the bathroom, bathe themselves, and other daily living skills. Usually, a professional job in psychology requires at least a Master's degree if not a doctoral degree." It sounded like a confession.

"Then why don't you get that?" he bluntly asked.

I elaborated on my reasoning that I was tired of school and burned out from studying textbooks. I was eager to start working for a living so I could get out from under my parent's roof. Then I asked him if he had a job. He smirked and said, "Yeah, I have a temporary job at the Kodak factory while I finish my six-year program in Engineering."

Then an amazing thing happened. Michaels volunteered information, "I think they're hiring new people now if you're interested."

"Well, yeah, sure," I said excitedly.

Michaels smiled a bit, "I don't know why you are getting so excited. It's just a factory job."

"I'm ready to take anything at this point. How do you know they have openings?"

"That's the thing, see. Kodak just lost a lawsuit for patent infringement of the Polaroid instant camera. They had to pay Polaroid hundreds of millions of dollars. So, to make up for the financial loss, Kodak cut everybody's pay from $8 to $5.50 an hour, which is just above minimum wage."

"That sucks," I empathized.

"You could say morale is down throughout the factory and a lot of people just up and quit. So, there you go, if you're interested," Michaels said nonchalantly.

"It's still better than nothing," I said as we walked onto the court and batted the ball back and forth.

After the weekend, I went to the Kodak factory to fill out and submit an employment application. To my surprise, the film developing giant called me back for an interview, which led to my hiring to work in film processing.

My first lesson in the "real world" was that contacts can be the difference in acquiring new opportunities.

***

When I showed up to work, I noticed that among the hundred or so workers there, I was about the youngest, fresh-faced employee. Several work areas were designated for each stage of film processing. I was assigned to a station where I would receive a tub full of different undeveloped film cartridges. My assignment was to attach each roll of film to a cardboard box that matched the type of film that was in the cartridge. The various types of cardboard boxes would enable the film developers to know which chemicals to use to develop the cartridges.

As easy as that was, the harder it became over time. Endless tubs of diverse film cartridges came my way like piles of mail to a mail sorter. Except if I attached the wrong cardboard box to the film, the development of the film would fail, thereby ruining the film and disappointing consumers eager to receive their photos of family, friends, and exotic trips. After a long, repetitive duration of this monotony, my concentration would surely ebb, and a mistake would ensue.

I wanted to work. Anything was better than unemployment, lying on the family couch, and getting ribbed for a lack of purpose. But here I was attaching rolls of film onto cardboard, without once calling on my past textbook studies about the physiology of the brain or statistical analysis for a research study. No written paper was required now. I just functioned physically roll after roll of film. As contrasting as this job was to my past academia, I felt even more foolish when the supervisor called me into her office to ask me why I matched the wrong box to the wrong film cartridge, thereby rendering the film useless. I had no explanation. I looked back at her without a clue as to an adequate defense for my error. I just apologized and, with no real conviction, claimed I would be more careful.

My second real world lesson was that a college education was not applicable to assembly line work.

The other workers exhibited jaded attitudes since receiving a three-dollar-an-hour pay cut as a result of the lawsuit with Polaroid. Yet they clung to their jobs. They were still better off than standing in an unemployment line. Most of the employees were men and women who depended on their meager wages to sustain their affairs just above the poverty line. There was a general feeling of paranoia that each would be fired and replaced by a young, fresh face like me, who could do the same work for less money. The other employees treated me with disdain as if I violated the territory of a wolf pack.

I worked throughout the summer at Kodak, but still scoured the daily want ads in *The Washington Post*. Towards the end of August, one classified ad screamed out from the paper, "Earn $20,000 a year salary, no experience necessary." That's perfect I thought. Twenty grand is double what I'm making now and the word "salary" seemed to have so much more gravitas than the word "wage" as if I were to enter a new socio-economic class, from blue collar to white collar. And "no experience necessary" was just too perfect to pass up. This was my big break.

I called the number on the want ad and the representative invited me to an orientation meeting along with 20 other prospective candidates. At the meeting, the company, Universal Learning, introduced themselves and their product, encyclopedias. Their pitch was that they were not only encyclopedias, but the set from A to Z came with a service that would provide up to the minute updates on any subject, so that the information was always current.

Given that it was the year 1986, a good seven years before the Internet came to public use, the concept of getting "up to the minute" information seemed revolutionary. The investment in the set of encyclopedias would never go out of date. The job of Encyclopedia Salesman was offered to anybody who agreed to attend a two-week training regimen. I was ecstatic. I put in my two weeks' notice at Kodak and happily attended the sales training with Universal Learning.

As expected, a classroom of 15 or so others attended the training. We sat through lectures of the history of the company, their values, and mission. We listened attentively as they described situations and how we should present the product and services. They went through various scenarios and how to deal with objections, and finally the almighty contract that would solidify the sale.

At first exposure, their marketing strategies seemed ingenious. They targeted young families who would want their kids to grow up with information about the world at their fingertips. That seemed logical, yet, I would later conclude, they targeted young families to exploit their naiveté to deal with pressure sales tactics. We were told to lessen the impact of the total cost of the encyclopedias, which would ultimately cost about $1,800 by stating that it would cost "as little as a Coke a day." What we were not supposed to let on was that it would take years to pay off the debt, which was the last thing a young couple needed while trying to get established.

Even more devious, the corporate representative explained that we should get a commitment when we were presenting the products in their homes while they were excited about it. We were told that in the state of Maryland, consumers had a three day right of rescission to back out of any contractual obligation. And this clause was part of the contract. This company, however, trained us to cover the words "Right of Rescission" with our thumb as we obtained the consumer's signature on the dotted line. As telling as this unethical practice was to keep the consumer ignorant of their rights, I thought that I would simply not engage in that particular method to close the sale.

Life Lesson 3: Rely on your conscience during an ethical dilemma.

At the completion of the two-week training program, it was time for us to sign a contract to accept their offer of employment.

Each one of us was called into a small room one at a time to finalize employment.

After a short time, it was my turn to enter the small room. I sat down as did the manager with a table between us. He reiterated the terms of employment as was advertised but indicated that I had a "choice" to elect the $20,000 a year salary or choose to work for commission. Well, that seemed to be an easy choice for me. Why not be guaranteed twenty grand a year? I put forth my election confidently, "I'll take the salary."

The manager took in my answer as if he had to swallow it before moving on. He looked at me and explained, "You know, you could make a lot, a lot more money through commissions." He went on to say, "In fact, we will drive you just as hard if you are salaried, but you won't realize the same financial rewards as you would through commissions."

"I know," I said, but I didn't know how many sales I would make. What if I didn't sell very much or anything at all. This may sound defeatist, but I was in uncharted territory. I had never sold anything before. At least if I were salaried, I would be paid no matter what happened. The guarantee seemed more appealing than unlimited but unrealized potential. So, after a moment of reflection, I came to the same conclusion. "I still think the salary would be better for me." The manager stood up abruptly and said that he'll have to consult with the owner of the business and for me to wait for his answer. He seemed a little flustered, but I was sure of my choice and felt relaxed while I waited.

After a few minutes, the owner, a large beer-bellied man with a bald head came in and repeated what the manager said verbatim. That seemed silly to me. If I was so sure of myself with the manager, what had changed other than the person "explaining" my "choice" to me? I reiterated, "I think I want the salary."

The owner, who had not taken the time to sit down, threw up his hands and abruptly walked out yelling at his manager "Get this guy out of here!"

Life Lesson 4: Know when a choice is not a real choice.

Life Lesson 5: If I had agreed to their terms, it would have been the first of a long list of disappointments.

I lost the job opportunity. During my drive all the way home, I was crestfallen. I felt as if I was close to my first professional, salaried job, but blew it. Now I was again a jobless interloper.

Back at square one, I sheepishly returned to the family home with the unsettling news that I would wake up tomorrow with no job, no agenda, nothing to show for myself. After retelling the sequence of events that resulted in my dismissal, my father reassured me that I didn't miss out on anything. "Those types of jobs are always available." Immediately my disappointment lifted. Then with his next breath he encouraged me to pursue real estate sales. I dismissed the idea immediately, feeling betrayed that he, being an administrative scientist, didn't suggest something of equal caliber to his own successful path as a professional. So as usual the communication between us broke down with his unintentional impact on me. I, like a sensitive bruise, interpreted his suggestion for another commission-based job as a disparaging assessment of my ability and unrealized talents.

The days turned to weeks and weeks into months where I did little more than scan the want ads and cursed the Catch 22 situation of not having experience necessary to get experience. All throughout this period, my father kept bringing up real estate as a possibility. Each time he did, I cringed and ignored him until I finally acquiesced and said, "Fine, I will take the real estate course while I look for a real job." I felt what the hell, at least I'll be preoccupied, and it will keep Dad quiet. I had supposed that a real estate license may be a good back up plan in the event I ever got a good job and lost it. I could always fall back on real estate sales. So, with the enthusiasm of a kid going to religious school, I enrolled in a six-week course to learn about the field of real estate sales.

2 In Pursuit of the Elusive First Professional Job

In the real estate class, I was all too comfortable as a student, which evoked nothing but self-doubt. I listened to the instructor explain real estate and mortgage lending practices, laws, and ethics. After the six weeks came and went, I took both the class test and the test for the real estate license, all of which were prerequisites to become a Realtor®. Accustomed to taking multiple choice tests from four years of college, I found it relatively easy to pass both tests. Now I had the credentials to sell real estate and just needed to get hired at one of the plethora of local real estate brokerages: Shannon & Luchs, Long & Foster, Coldwell Banker, Century 21, and many other small, individual brokerage houses.

Although I never intended to actually practice selling real estate, I believed having the license would be a good back up plan should I ever have a real job and lose it. But then I thought, what good is possessing a license if I don't have any experience. So, with no other job prospects, I simply walked into a branch office and asked whether they were hiring, filled out an application, and left it in their hands to contact me if they were interested. After submitting applications to several different branches, I returned home and resumed my throne of leisure. It wasn't long before, the phone rang, and I was called in for an interview. I didn't have a resume, since I never had any professional work history, and I didn't think my former teen work experiences washing cars and flipping pizzas, nor my most recent experience connecting film cartridges to boxes would impress anyone. So, I winged it and just showed up to interview at a New Millennium Realty office about a mile away from my family home.

Personally, I was hard pressed to believe anyone would be interested in hiring me until I learned that the job was 100 percent sales commission. The motto being, "you make as much as you're worth." They would provide me with a desk, phone, office, all the necessary contracts and addenda, and hold weekly meetings to teach us about closing skills, writing contingencies, and marketing strategies. I learned that the common amount for a commission was six percent; however, that was divided amongst the listing and buying brokers, which split the commission in two, leaving three percent to be split again between my broker and me.

Single-family detached homes averaged about $100,000 in my county during the mid-1980s. I began to calculate: six percent of $100,000 is $6,000. Split between the selling and buying brokers left $3,000, which was split again between me and my broker. I would only realize $1,500. Still the opportunity to make serious money remained up to me.

I would also learn the downside of a fully commissioned real estate job. Not only was a payday dependent on making a sale, but I would have to invest months with customers looking for the right home and a couple more months waiting for the buyers to secure a loan.

Making matters more precarious, buyers often relied on selling their current home in order to use the equity to buy their next, larger, more expensive home. I would learn this situation to be a "contingency." The buyers must sell their home within an allotted period or the contract falls by the wayside, and everyone goes home without a payday. A lot of time and effort into the process was no guarantee of a paycheck. This commission arrangement seemed to me to be somewhat of a sham, which was why so many brokers would take a chance and hire someone like me. To them it was a numbers game. They never knew which real estate agent would emerge a top seller and bring in the dollars. So, the minor expense to hire an agent was worth the promise of a sales bonanza.

Soon I would learn that contract contingencies and loan approvals were not the only obstacles to securing a payday. I would have to establish relationships with complete strangers, research houses for specific amenities, explain market conditions, manage buyer anxieties and unrealistic expectations. After all, home ownership was one of the largest investments of most people's lives. And there were a lot of potential pitfalls to this investment. Certain homes were more like money pits than investments: homes facing major highways, homes next to railroad tracks, or bordering land that would be later transformed into some obnoxious industrial enterprise. There were flood zones to worry about, black mold, excessive radon, lead paint, termites, and a host of other disasters to a homeowner, which may not have an easy remedy.

New buyers expected a resale home to be in perfect condition. One buyer even eyed the drywall of one home I showed, and he complained that the walls were crooked. But it was my job to convert objections into enthusiastic sales commitments.

Life Lesson 6: Learning about any field is another education that can potentially help you throughout the rest of your life.

I got a haircut so that my lush hair quaffed back out of my face and revealed my forehead and ears. And with the help of my father's competence at wearing suits, he led me to buy the appropriate clothing and even showed me how to tie a Windsor knot.

Life Lesson 7: Fathers always know more about convention than recent college graduates.

I was transformed into a professional, who happened to have the occasional acne flareup and a bony ribcage of a young, thin man. My dad gave me his old briefcase, which at first, held nothing but my lunch, and I was ready to go. Go where was a different issue.

***

The real estate office was situated in a historic house in the middle of Gaithersburg, Maryland. It had a reception desk, manager's office, an octagonal room with six desks, and the broker's office, which was adorned with plaques of achievement for high sales volume from various agents who worked there over the years. Trophies from various sporting events proudly displayed on the mantel from teams the broker, Mr. Kent, sponsored. Articles from newspapers were clipped and framed showcasing the many times Mr. Kent was recognized for his good works supporting the church, food drives, elderly care, and many other charitable contributions. His office was a shrine for his good works supporting humanity and the community. Mr. Kent took his reputation seriously and expected as much from his crew of agents. To Mr. Kent, his reputation and community standing was the driving force to his financial success.

About 12 agents in all shared the desks and came and left the office as needed. We agents made our own office hours and worked as hard or little as desired. After all, the broker wasn't paying anything for our association but welcomed half the commission from each sale from his agents.

Most of the agents were middle to senior-aged, divorced women. A female gay couple. One married woman. One thirty-something man, one young man just out of high school, and me, the recent college graduate full of textbook knowledge.

Fran and Lilly were the senior-aged and butch-looking gay couple who always seemed to be working with the most extremely difficult real estate cases: land deals, historical buildings, demolition, and reconstruction, and so forth. They were always hunting for special permits and researching esoteric laws and seemingly always getting into hot water for one reason or another. Fran was also a special needs teacher, but they both were committed to life of wheeling and dealing in real estate. They lived and breathed real estate negotiations, closing contracts and getting embroiled in near lawsuits over one dispute or another. Somehow, they managed securing these odd contracts and eked out a living together.

Marylyn was the attractive and married middle-aged woman who didn't depend on commissions because her husband was gainfully employed as a senior administrator for the National Institutes of Health. But she scrambled for contracts so she could pull her own weight in the family. She was one of the leading sales agents.

Chuck was a blue-collar type in his thirties with little to show for his age, living in the garage of his parent's home. He was a large man, with little strands of brown hair on the top of his balding head and a thick brown mustache. Chuck had a soft tone and, despite only having a high-school education, learned everything he could about real estate. As if to compensate for his lack of college, he educated everyone he came into contact with every facet of real estate as possible. As I would later learn…

Life Lesson 8: Sales is about providing some information so long as its relevant and important, but the sales agent's purpose isn't to simply educate, but rather obtain a commitment to buy or sell.

Chuck, the poor guy, had a heart of pillow feathers, but constantly wasted his time on educating rather than selling.

Bryce was the other new kid in the office, just out of high school. New agents like Bryce and me held great promise, but always deferred to the rest of the office. They were not only our elders but had an abundance of experience and history of success. Bryce and I were just a hope for something to develop. We were generally ignored by the adults in the office who depended on their commissions as a lifeline for financial independence.

Bryce and I really did not have anything in common with the elders. They had a couple of decades of work experience, families, kids, houses and real adult challenges. Bryce and I still lived in our family's homes and did not share any of the financial pressures of the elders.

Life Lesson 9: Trying to sell a product that one can't afford for oneself is a life on the edge of hypocrisy and incredulity.

Most of the other agents were bitter, divorced women who were surviving on commissions to subsist without a husband's second income. These women learned the ropes and competed viciously. And many converted their controlling behavior into $100,000 yearly incomes. These gals had the entire package. They were young enough to use their alure to captivate their customers and bitchy enough to push them around and close the deals. They often had kids so their sales were their livelihood, which would not be denied. The sales agent landscape was dominated by women who either depended solely on commissions or were married and could relax to the sales pressures. After all, from the time an agent established a contact through the time it took to reach settlement, many months would have passed, all for a $1,500 or so paycheck. The only way to make a living was to seriously hustle, charm, and close the deals.

Gertrude, the German spinster who chain smoked into her old age, had been a real estate agent in her younger years. She had all the confidence of her earlier success. But now she was an old pruned lady, whose voice had been smoked into a nearly incomprehensible grovel. Her production was near nil and whenever she had a client, she seemed to cater to their every whim until even she realized her clients were what the industry called "sight seers," a couple posing as customers only to get the royal, free treatment to see homes they could never afford. But to sightseers, it was a fun outing at the expense of an overly eager, yet careless agent who failed to prequalify them.

Life Lesson 10: Always obtain prerequisite information to know who is a valid customer/client before spending your time and effort unnecessarily.

As I would later learn, an agent was always supposed to gather their customer's income and debt information to assess their potential to secure the loan. This practice was known as "pre-qualifying."

The office manager, Sherry, was a large, obese woman who resented that she made the lion's share of income over her deadbeat husband. She had a long history in real estate and claimed it was in her blood. She was nice enough but was never at a loss to criticize underperformances or questionable ethics of her flock of agents. She was the one who worried about potential lawsuits against the brokerage. She was somewhat the conscience of the agency.

The broker, Mr. Kent, worked in the back room, and was rarely seen, like the wizard behind the curtain. He emerged only when a sale occurred. After a sales contract was ratified, he directed the office manager to write the responsible agent's name and sales price of the property on a chalkboard, keeping a running tally for each month. The other times he emerged from obscurity was when the collective sales total from the office was nowhere near the million dollars per month he required. After all, his 1.5 percent share of a million-dollar sales volume was $15,000 while each agent was lucky to get a single sale per month.

Life Lesson 11: The real money was in being a broker who earned money off the labor of agents who desperately scrambled to make a buck.

Mr. Kent's success relied on the production of the office as a whole. He didn't care if an agent was a poor producer so long as that agent sold something during the year. Other more successful agents would make up the difference by selling millions of dollars worth of real estate. In fact, if an agent's accumulative sales volume over a single year reached a million dollars, they earned a prestigious plaque and new business cards indicating they were a million-dollar agent. Little did the public know, a million in real estate sales entailed selling about ten to fifteen houses and resulted in a mere $15,000 income for the agent.

Life Lesson 12: Image of success isn't necessarily success.

But here I was one of the few college-educated agents, with no experience in real estate or for that matter anything else. I was expected to establish relationships with complete strangers who were all much older than me. They ranged from newlyweds looking for their starter home to families moving across the country to families looking for larger homes, and of course, the myriad of divorcés who not only had to sell their current home but also look for an affordable replacement home. In the mid-1980s, the market was popping with all kinds of reasons people were selling their homes and buying new ones. And as the mortgage rates declined, housing prices soared, which caused people to jump at the chance to buy real estate. Unwittingly, my timing for entry into the real estate industry couldn't have been better.

***

The office personnel all seemed nice enough, if one could forgive the unspoken treachery of jealousy just beneath the surface. If anyone closed a sale, congratulations were easily doled out, with a suppression of seething envy. But the envy and jealousy were the secrets that powered competition among the sales crew. I seemed to slip under the radar as

I was young and unproven. Most likely I would come and leave the agency as fast as a changing interest rate. Many people entered the real estate industry looking to cherry pick the easy money. They were part timers who boosted their annual income with a couple of sales per year. Or they hung their license as a proud member of the agency, only to quit after a few months of effort with nothing to show for it.

Life Lesson 13: Most people can't work for nothing for very long.

In fact, most of the agents offered advice, especially Chuck, who couldn't resist talking about the difference between success and failure, yet rarely brought in a ratified contract (signed by both buyer and seller).

Since most of the other agents were already busy working with current contacts, I volunteered to answer the office phones from callers who were new on the scene, whereby I would attempt to establish an agent customer relationship. When the phone didn't ring, it was up to me to make cold calls, outgoing calls, to random persons in the hopes I would call someone who happened to be looking to buy or sell a home and who wasn't already working with an agent. Cold calls were despised by the veteran agents because there was a very small success rate and a lot of painful, angry rejections by those we unnecessarily disturbed during their dinner time or care for their crying babies, and so forth.

Agents had at their disposal various marketing ways to gain clients: they made cold calls, sent out mass mailings, canvassed neighborhoods in person, conducted seminars, advertised in homes magazines and newspapers, sent out promotional items, and held open houses, anything to get names and phone numbers of potential clients. Since I didn't have much knowledge of these tactics and less gumption than I should have had, as well as, no financial resources from which to draw, I was relegated to the drudgery of making that one percent success rate by calling hundreds of persons randomly.

Before I had a chance to make a single cold call, the phone rang. I answered, "New Millennium Realty, this is Roy C. Luschman. How can I help you?" The first real trick of the trade that I learned was to ask not "may I help you," but rather "how may I help you," to immediately get to the purpose of the call. If I learned anything at all about any sales job is that they employ a myriad of manipulative methods, especially using language to encourage sales. It's said in the industry, you were always closing a sale, even from the beginning of introductions. I was told never to call a sales contract "a contract," because people are inhibited to engage in a legally binding documentation. The connotations of the word "contract" scared people. Therefore, we were told to use the synonym "agreement" in its place. For advertisements, words such as "quaint," "cute," or "cozy" replaced "small."

While I understood the psychology behind these types of manipulations, I didn't care for them. I reluctantly went along with the more innocuous ones such as "alternative choice questions:" "Would you like the newly built house or the vintage historical home?" Either way, the question is designed to obtain a commitment to buy something. But frankly, I didn't think I would fool anyone by calling a contract an agreement. I worked in Montgomery County, Maryland, one of the most educated counties in America. The home buyers weren't door stoppers. They understood the basics.

The real estate industry did understand that most people are inhibited from committing to buy the most expensive item of their lives. And because of this inhibition, customers often create flimsy objections to defeat the process. "I don't want this house because the kitchen wallpaper is hideous." It was a game of psychology whereby the agent was to convert objections into a commitment.

Coming from an academic setting, I viewed real estate from an intellectual point of view. I quickly understood the financial advantages of locking in a low interest rate for the loan; the tax deductions that would lower the tax bill, and of course appreciation, the typical increases in value of the property. And perhaps the most important concept was leveraging money: using a 3% down payment to buy a $100,000 house. Thereby with only $3,000, you would be getting the benefit of the annual increase in value of your $100,000 home.

The counter argument of course is that you have to pay a monthly mortgage, which consists of principle, interest, taxes, and insurance (PITI). But you have to live somewhere, why not pay a monthly mortgage rather than rent, where you don't get the benefits of tax deductions as well as appreciation? Afterall by the time the mortgage is paid off, the home value may triple, whereas renters have nothing but rental receipts to show for that time.

Like I was saying the intellectual argument was persuasive and logical to me. I had no problem reiterating it to every prospect who came along. But what I found out was…

Life Lesson 14: Many, if not most, people make financial decisions based on emotions, and those emotions may not consider logical benefits.

So, despite the air-tight arguments of the financial benefits and rewards of homeownership, the prospective buyer of a home may reject the perfect purchase because they didn't like the color of the carpeting. No matter the fact that carpeting is an easily changeable cosmetic issue. To the buyer, the colors of a home may remind them of a negative memory or association with a former family home. To them, it's not a cosmetic, temporary, issue, it's the color of the room that conjures up the nightmare childhood when he heard mom and dad screaming at each other in the canary yellow kitchen.

The corollary is the same. Sometimes customers buy something for the most ridiculously illogical reasons. Some prospective homebuyers fall in love with a home because of the cosmetic elements, such as the moon-shaped window on top of the door.

To take this even further, sometimes a customer decided whether to buy or not buy based on the emotions evoked from the real estate agent. In other words, if the agent was enthusiastic about a prospective home, the customer may follow suit like an imprinted duckling following the first thing it comes into contact after hatching. If the duckling saw a dog, as far as the duckling was concerned the dog was his parent.

Life Lesson 15: People commonly follow the lead of a sales agent based on the agent's enthusiasm more than the receipt of relevant information.

That's what Chuck didn't understand. He was overcompensating for his academic insecurities by trying to educate the customers with a deluge of unwanted information. While the customer may be impressed, at some point they stop listening or can't keep up and find themselves in a state of confusion, and ultimately reluctant to buy anything. Chuck mastered real estate information, but was more of an educator than successful sales agent.

More importantly, Life Lesson 16: The agent shouldn't impose their own prejudices upon the prospective buyers.

If the buyers think a run-down dump is the ideal fixer upper, that is their prerogative. They may like to renovate and capitalize on a lower sales price, even if the agent does not favorably see it that way. To other people, the more pristine a house, the better. There are fewer repair and maintenance expenses.

Every home buyer has certain reservations, or conditions that must be met for an agreement to transpire. In the real estate industry, those demands are called contingencies. The real estate agent is supposed to be literate enough to write those contingencies on an addendum so that they are legally enforceable. Translating a purchaser's demands in writing entailed the art of listening and then articulating the concept before writing a contingency using legal jargon. This can be intimidating to many agents, most of whom didn't have a college education.

For some reason, writing felt natural to me. I had taken numerous writing classes and the use of legal jargon came easily to me. I read the county approved contract for home sales, as well as a legal guide. I was fairly immersed in the process of real estate sales, but had yet worked with any real customers. So, I continued to learn from the weekly manager's sessions, which touched upon a different topic each week: closing skills, contracts, marketing, ethics, and so on.

The ethics in the industry were freakish to me. We were told that since the sellers were responsible for paying our commissions, we owed our allegiance to them. That sounded simple enough, the buyers would obtain our services for free. Seems like everybody wins. However, the listing agent who represents the seller was typically not the one who finds the buyer. The two main ways of obtaining a commission were to either list a house to sell or find a buyer to buy a house listed on the multiple listing service. If the listing agent found his own buyer without the help of another agent, the listing agent and her broker share the whole six percent commission. Otherwise, the commission was split between the selling broker and the buying broker.

The freaky part was that if I carted around potential buyers to see homes for months on end and finally find one they want to buy, I'd have established an emotional relationship with them. The customers would think that I was their agent, as if I do everything to protect them and get them the best deal–when the opposite allegiance was the case. According to the real estate industry, I owed my allegiance to the sellers, people who I may never have even met. So, when buyers asked, "How much should I bid," hoping for me to tell them "You could save yourselves $10,000 by bidding 90 percent of the asking price," I must "ethically" say "Since the sellers are paying the commission, I work for the seller. All I can do is say that a full price offer would give you the best chance of ratifying the contract." And if the buyers felt slighted and decided to go away and buy another house with another agent, all the time and effort spent with those buyers was lost with nothing to show for it.

The "ethics" seemed backward to me. The dilemma reminded me of a question I had to write an essay for as a freshman in college.

The question was, "Should you obey an unjust law?" Little did I know, I would actually have to face the hypothetical in a real-life situation.

3   The Real World

Although I wore a suit and tie, coiffed my hair, and came to an office daily, I somehow felt short of being in the real world, just yet. I wasn't actually getting paid. Or at least, I hadn't realized any payment for my participation. I had to pay my dues, so to speak, and perform some grunge work.

I came into the office and assumed telephone duty, which entailed answering calls and making cold calls. Many of the agents shunned telephone duty thinking it was a waste of time. But how else to obtain new clients if one hadn't engaged in years of shameless self-promotion to establish a deep backlog of contacts? I didn't have a single contact. That changed when the phone rang, and I established a dialogue with Francis who called from Georgia and was looking to move to Maryland. She was a 25-year-old who prided herself as an editor. She landed a job at a local newspaper in Montgomery County, Maryland. Francis was ready to invest in a single-family detached home, the American dream. After all, she just secured a job in one of the richest counties in the country.

Chuck overheard my phone call and immediately weighed in, "The problem with the out-of-state customers is that the home values and salaries vary greatly from state to state. People coming from low cost of living states can't afford Montgomery County's cost of living." Montgomery County, Maryland bordered Washington DC and had one of the highest expenses in the country. Francis was from Georgia, one of the lowest cost-of-living regions. She stated her terms "I'm looking for a single-family detached home with a den, two car garage, large kitchen. My budget is $50,000." It was at this disclosure of her budget that my jaw dropped. While $50,000 was an appropriate sum to purchase a house in Georgia, in Montgomery County that amount would only buy a doghouse or an outhouse. Most single-family detached houses started at $100,000, and even at that would only get one that was in need of a lot of repair and maintenance or would be in a poor neighborhood. I tried to convey that to her in more diplomatic terms;

however, she was adamant that if I wanted to work with her, I was to find her this house.

I gathered her financial information and calculated her income to debt ratios. Then, I scoured the multiple listing service computer searching for a house that cheap and only found some in the worst, crime-ridden neighborhoods. Chuck laughed at my efforts and lectured me, "You are wasting your time, Roy, with this unrealistic customer." Then he goaded, "But go ahead, spin your wheels. Maybe you'll learn something from it."

After a month in the business and nothing to show for it, the day of my appointment with Francis finally came. I anxiously awaited the appointment at 1:00 pm. When she didn't show, I was disappointed. I had spent an abundance of time researching all the lowest cost homes and driving to each of them so I would know where to go when chauffeuring Francis. I also went inside the dozen or so homes to match the amenities she found desirable. I took into account her commute distance, the proximity to shopping and recreation, etc. I knew her

$50,000 budget was incongruent with the probable real cost of $100,000 or so. Townhouses were of course much cheaper than the single-family detached houses, but Francis was specific and somewhat fanatic about what she wanted.

So, there I was with my twenty pages of home details, maps, and notes from hours of previewing the houses, and making arrangements with the listing agent to show the properties to Francis on a given day and time. All for naught.

As I waited two hours past the appointment time for Francis, I could telepathically hear the jeers inside the other agents' heads. "I told you so. You are wasting your time." Then a call came in. It was Francis. She sounded perturbed and said that she had just been with another real estate agent, and complained that she showed her the worst houses in the "worst" neighborhoods. But what further infuriated Francis was that this other agent tried to sell her a townhouse. Without any apology or acknowledgement that she had been disloyal, she said that she wanted to give me a try. She then wanted to see me within the hour.

Despite her ditching me for someone else and nearly wasting all my time and effort, I withheld my contempt. After all, there was no requirement that she do business with anyone other than who she chooses. There was no contract between us binding her to maintain an allegiance with me until a sales contract was actually signed and accepted by the sellers and listing agent. Then I realized, the other agent must have shown her the properties that I had prepared to show her. After all, the agents from all the different brokerages used the same Multiple Listing Service (MLS) to research properties for sale. The MLS is one database used by all competing agents, so we all have the same list of homes to show. Despite salvaging my only customer, how was I to do anything different? That's why the emotional bond with a customer was so important.

Life Lesson 17: The relationship between customer and agent is built on trust and loyalty. And the trust and loyalty of a given customer is based on establishing a relationship.

The relationship begins with rapport, which is not limited to imparting an abundance of information like Chuck does. Sometimes it's the small talk and the ability to relate on a personal level, coupled with the necessary amount of optimism and enthusiasm that gets an agent to that trust and loyalty level with a customer.

A rain shower began and it was late afternoon, when a wet, bedraggled Francis came blustering into the New Millennium Realty office. She was worn out from her trip from Georgia and frustrated from the first agent who didn't show her what she wanted.

Despite being diminutive, Francis was a feisty twenty-something ready to set the world ablaze. And one of her desires was to own her first home. She thought of herself as a tough-nosed editor who fixed other people's errors. She was hard to convince, but after I stated the facts that no matter who she consulted, the same properties would await her rejection, she reluctantly agreed to see some townhouses.

Life Lesson 18: Sometimes the stark, ugly truth is the most persuasive.

Off we went in my Toyota Corolla, a hand-me-down car from my parents. She sat in the passenger's seat and the godawful attempt to make small talk became nearly unbearable. She was reticent and I pelted her with questions that made me feel as if I were on a first date. We were about the same age; however, I could only imagine us a couple as a weird fantasy. In reality, we were barely able to exchange words. But it was my job to break down barriers.

As I pulled onto the main drag in Gaithersburg, she did manage to muster a question, "Is the neighborhood safe?" I reassured her that the entire county was one of the richest in the nation. Just then sirens could be heard from what seemed like all directions. Soon a twenty-car backup obscured the disturbance where the ambulance and police vehicles converged. I cringed at every searing high pitch of the sirens and passage of speeding police vehicles. I thought, this certainly doesn't look good. This will scare Francis. I had just reassured her. I must have sounded like a lying hypocrite.

We waited in the car as the line of vehicles slowly circumvented the scene. Eventually my car passed the grisly site. A man lay sprawled on the asphalt dead. He had been struck by an oncoming vehicle. The tension in my car was palpable. We silently watched the medics lift the dead man onto a gurney.

The mood in the car was solemn, but we continued toward a townhouse that promised to deliver me into the real world. It just started out inauspiciously.

***

The early evening soon became dark as we entered the last of three townhomes that I showed Francis. It was a unique corner unit that had a balcony overlooking a courtyard. It even had a den outside the master bedroom. It was in marvelous condition.

As I tried to close the deal, I warned, "homes as inexpensive as this one, in this good a condition, will go quickly." But instead of motivating her to commit, I probably sounded as if I was disingenuously trying to pressure her to buy. But in reality, the market was what was considered a "seller's market." That meant, many more buyers were looking for homes than were available. As a result of this seller's market, home prices were soaring, increasing in value every month, and listings didn't stay on the market for long. It was common for several competing offers to be submitted at the same time. And that's exactly what happened.

As fatigued as Francis was from her trek and full day of disappointing home searching, she reluctantly agreed to submit a contract offer, but not without negotiating. So, the offer was low. Consequently, when multiple offers came in that night, her contract was not picked and we all went home disappointed. I felt as if I were close to my first sale, but the rug was yanked from beneath me and rolled up and beaten with it. The sale seemed within reach, but the work I put in was for naught.

I contacted Francis the next day and we began another tour of a new string of homes. The home we lost out on was quite unique and we were unlikely to find another with a den, balcony and courtyard all in perfect condition and freshly painted with new carpet. Despite the reset in our outing, the loss of the "perfect" home soured her ambition and suddenly none of the new listings we saw were good enough.

Life Lesson 19: Emotional states affect perception; perception affects motivation.

I attempted to address her situation so she would be more receptive. But as much as I understood the problem, my solution had little to do with emotions. Instead, I did a "Chuck." I harped on the benefits of home ownership and the soaring prices that will make it even more difficult to buy in the future. But that was all logic and information. Now was the time, she could be a homeowner and build equity quickly as the value increased by the day. My idea of an emotional connection sadly seemed to start and stop at the selling of the intellectual argument made of numbers and benefits, appreciation, tax deductions, lowering mortgage rates and points, and whatever else I learned from a textbook about the facts and figures of the real estate transaction.

After showing about the eighth townhouse, Francis' mood changed simply from the elapse of time. Nothing I said had much of an affect, in that my repetitive factual messages must have lost an audience by midday. It was now the late afternoon on a Sunday. She must have felt the pressure she imposed on herself to get settled in preparation for her new job in a new state. Excellent market conditions and people's own motivation seemed to compensate for my nebbish social skills.

We entered a townhouse in Montgomery Village, a planned community. Despite what I internally considered somewhat an uninspiring townhouse, Francis took interest in the home. She could visualize it as her hovel. To my surprise, she committed to buying it at full price, $62,000. That night, I gave her the news that the sellers agreed to the contractual terms and the agreement began. Of course, the process involved that all the parties jump through hoops of barbed wire.

Francis now had to obtain her loan, the house had to pass termite, radon, and mechanical inspections; and the appraisal had to meet or be higher than the agreed upon sales price. The parties would have to show up at settlement and everyone had to sign a half inch thick set of disclosure papers before the deal was actually done. That would consume another 60 days. But as far as my broker was concerned, it was a firm deal, and the value of the home sale, the address, and my name would be written on the chalkboard. This procedure had practical implications to keep a running tally of sales, so the broker knew where he stood on expected income. It also was a sign of prestige designed to motivate the other agents who had not yet generated any sales.

There my name was, chalked on the board along with the highest sales agents in the office. Their names appeared multiple times for houses of far greater value, but I made my mark, cracking the enigmatic code of sales and on my way to earning my first professional paycheck. I was aware that the six percent commission would be divided twice, first between my broker and the selling broker, and then again between my broker and me, leaving me one and a half percent of $62,000 or $930 dollars. At the calculation of this figure, I was flying high which supercharged my gumption to seek more sales.

I received several congratulations, regardless of sincerity. The other agents had to nibble their words a bit. Though my sale was not a huge deal, I converted an unlikely customer who was discarded by everyone else into a sale through persistence. The other agents seemed to deal with their incredulity by laughing off my sale and attributing it to luck.

Life Lesson 20: Success takes luck, but successful people put themselves in positions to be lucky.

4 The Sales Challenge

In the case of cold calls, agents called unsuspecting persons and simply asked whether they were interested in buying or selling a home. Most people weren't, but a predictable, small percentage of persons were just at the point of thinking about such a move. For every hundred calls, an agent may connect with just one receptive person who was gung-ho and thankful that we are making the path to ownership so easy for them. It was a numbers game. All day long, agents made these "unwanted" calls to persons who exhibited a range of emotions from gung-ho to downright angry.

Life Lesson 21: To make something happen, you must disturb the status quo. In other words, you can make something happen by initiating action.

Life Lesson 22: A salesperson must have Kevlar skin to deflect harsh rejections.

As Chuck and the other agents relegated themselves to phone duty making tedious cold calls, I came into the office and perched myself at a vacant desk. "Going to make some cold calls, Roy?" Chuck smiled with guile, believing that if he had to make 100 calls just to land one client, I was going to be on the phones for much longer time than that. Internally, he took glee in watching me. He expected to watch me begin the calls with enthusiasm and slowly degenerate into a dejected state of frustration.

Chuck's belief of the pecking order in the office was first the veteran agents then me, the acned newbie. But all that shattered as I made a connection with my first outgoing call. Granted it was someone who was looking to rent not buy, and the potential commission was only about $150, but none the less I scheduled an immediate appointment to show him rentals. I felt he was a real customer, and I had no other better customers to work with. So why not? Chuck and the others were flabbergasted. They were used to spending hours on the phone handling rejection after rejection and here I come along and—on my first attempt—land a customer. I could hear them seething. It was as if the pecking order was unraveling into discordant chaos.

When my customer, David, came in to the office for his appointment, we exchanged introductions, and I asked him what he was looking for. He replied, "Oh, I just need a small place in the vicinity for myself. And a guest room for my two teenage boys. They visit every so often."

David volunteered, "I can pay about $700 per month for rent." Of course, before spending any more time with any customer, I prequalified him. This entailed asking a lot of personal financial questions. I bluntly asked him what was his annual salary and revolving monthly debts then calculated his income to debt ratios. Immediately, I realized he was a good candidate to not only rent a house, but he was equally qualified to secure a loan to buy a townhouse. So, I introduced the idea to him, saying, "For about the same amount per month as rent, you could own your own home." Then I elaborated on all the benefits of homeownership: appreciation, tax deductions, and the fact that a fixed mortgage doesn't increase every year like rent does. "That's cool with me," he said, receptive to the idea. I researched and showed David a bevy of townhouses and within hours, I had my second contract.

Life Lesson 23: Sometimes you can make something from what appears like nothing; you just have to try.

I had been a licensed realtor for a mere six weeks and already ratified two contracts for a combined contractual total of $132,000. As I manned the phones, incoming calls from persons looking to buy or sell a home sometimes landed in my pocket. The idea was that when such a call comes your way, which occurred about once every few hours, the agent handling the call must establish rapport and some sort of relationship, prequalify their finances, and pin down an appointment to set in motion the potential for a sale. Converting calls into appointments was the game. Somehow other agents let those occasional gifts slip through their grasp, while I somehow managed to recognize and collect these callers into a fine nest of golden eggs ready to hatch commissions.

As the weeks passed, I converted more callers into appointments, loyal relationships, and eventually sales. I was a bona fide real estate agent with an understanding of the fundamentals. I racked up sale after sale from customers buying townhouses and a few of the more expensive single-family houses.

I worked tirelessly, every day of the week. I had no finish to the day's work. If a customer could only see homes after 8:00 pm, I was there available to show them the latest homes. I opened lock boxes to vacant homes, late at night to address the needs of the customers. I worked on weekends, Saturday being the most popular day of the week for house showings. But my ambition didn't stop there, I gladly sacrificed my traditional interest in watching professional football games on Sunday to show more houses. I taxied customers throughout every inch of Montgomery County.

I showed condos in the thickest urban settings. I escorted potential home buyers to houses throughout suburbia and throughout the outskirts of rural parts of Northern Montgomery County. Some buyers wanted acreage surrounding their houses and to traverse old country roads, while others wanted to live in a family community with lots of small children playing about. Still others wanted to be in proximity to a parkland, a lake, a community athletic center, the business sector, schools, the town centers, the main highway. Some of the customers wanted their houses to face East toward Mecca. Others wanted a southern exposure for the sunlight.

There were old homes, new homes, foreclosures, fixer uppers, pristine houses, well landscaped, furnished, and vacant homes of various styles.

I also listed a few homes, which entailed holding open houses and advertising in homes' magazines. I studied how the expert top sales agents advertised their listings, which were usually $400,000 mansions. They used full-page advertisements with a flattering picture of the property accented with colorful verbiage describing the amenities. I noticed that the size of the ads corresponded with the value of the listing. The larger the ad the more expensive the house.

The few listings I had were mostly townhouses or small houses. The run-of-the-mill colonials, split-levels, split foyers, and ranchers were the cookie-cutter types of homes most common to the Washington Metropolitan region. To get a different type of architecture meant going somewhere else or buying a very old house. By the end of the year, my accumulative sales of houses surpassed $1,000,000. I was now in a class that was recognized by the industry with awards and a new business card indicating that I was a million-dollar agent. The other agents took notice. Fran and Lilly, both overweight, especially could be heard whining, "He's going to be rich, and he only has a 28-inch waist."

***

The pressures of earning commission sales showed on many furrowed brows of my colleagues. While they worried about paying steep mortgages and all the other costs of living in the adult world, I still enjoyed my run of sales while living in my parent's home rent free. Although many months passed until I saw a paycheck from a sale, I had so many consecutive sales that my paychecks were consistently received on a monthly basis and sometimes a few times in a single month. I was amassing more and more cash, collecting as much as $4,500 for a whopper sale of a $300,000 "McMansion" to a doctor and his finance. All I did was escort them to a new homes' development and showed them one of the model homes. The customers were ecstatic, and the home developer took care of all the inspections and details through to their settlement. Money felt as if it were falling from the vaulted ceilings.

Life Lesson 24: In sales, you earn as much as you're worth.

I felt as far away from being an assembly line worker at Kodak than ever before. I was making and accumulating real wealth. But at the age of 23, I pined to buy my own home. After finding dozens of homes for others, I wanted to seek out my own home. Afterall, who heard of someone selling real estate without owning any themselves?

The issue came up numerous times while escorting customers in my car. A customer would ask if I owned a property basically to see whether I had any personal experience in the product I was trying so hard to peddle. The lack of ownership always shone light on the dark cloud over my head. However, after a year and a half selling real estate, I had saved about $30,000. I needed about $15,000 more to place a generous down payment, with something left over for a few months of my mortgage.

I received a call from a Nigerian woman, Ababuo, and her husband, Abayomrunkoje. They had been renting and wanted a new place to live. I prequalified them and convinced them that for the same monthly rental amount, they could be paying a fixed mortgage as homeowners. I had seen this situation many times and knew how to convert them. I started to regularly show them small, older houses in Rockville.

During this period, I made contact with a young power couple, Edward and Carol, who worked for Rockwell Aeronautics. They were just marginally older than me, probably not even 30, yet they owned a $300,000 colonial and wanted to sell it to buy a house in the $600,000 range. They were technologists, working with mainframe computers for cutting-edge industry leaders. Edward was short man who overcompensated for his stature with smugness and arrogance. His wife, Carol, towered over Edward and was as chunky as a mainframe computer compared to him. They were both curt and sharp tongued with each other, demanding each other's respect by exhibiting competing airs of confidence. Why they were looking to advance their financial investments when divorce was inevitable in their future, I'll never know. Even I could foresee a vicious divorce as a corollary to their confidence. I would later realize they were litigious, petty, and only wanted to work with me because they thought they could easily beat up on me if a lawsuit should transpire.

Most of the clients were okay, even enjoyable. But this couple grated against my sensibilities. They bitched and sniped at each other at every chance. Yet the promise of potentially listing their home and selling them a McMansion was a great temptation and necessitated a phlegmatic approach.

Life Lesson 25: Place personal bias aside when conducting business.

Over the course of several months, I showed property after property. They were fastidious finding fault with not only every one of my utterances and with each other but also with every home I presented. Meanwhile, the national newscasters spoke more and more about a potential recession. The more the predictions were spoken, the more consumer confidence reacted, and the easy sales started drying up. The number of consumers became fewer and fewer, and the remaining ones still had inhibitions. Real estate agents were quitting by the droves.

I was still short the necessary finances to make the leap into homeownership and start leading my life without the crimping governance of my parent's house rules. My customer list dwindled to just a few reliables: the Nigerian couple and the annoying power couple, Carol and Edward. And the showings were taking months. The fast and easy sales were gone.

The perennial ethical dilemma of the sales agent arises when the agent wants to tell the customers the truth, but can't without jeopardizing the sale. For example, the Rockwell Aeronautical power couple, Edward and Carol. After I found them a house to buy, they anxiously wanted to know how fast I could sell their house. Obviously, they assumed I had some precise knowledge of the future that they didn't have. If one provided an accurate, truthful answer, it would be something like, "The sale of your home depends on market conditions, the showcasing and marketing of your home, and a little luck as to who wants your home." Some of those things such as showcasing and marketing a home was up to the sales agent's efforts, but who's to know what persons out in the world become aware of the listing, visit the listed house, and submits a favorable bid. At best the agent can take an educated guess on the time it takes to sell a house based on previous experience and market conditions, but ultimately, it's up to the gods when it will happen. And, the more expensive the home the fewer qualified buyers there are.

Although I was a million-dollar agent after my first year, I was still a little green with all the marketing and contacts. Listings were hard to sell in a soft market. So, what could I say, if the truth was too offensive to a homeowner? All I could muster was, "I am confident it will sell relatively fast if the price is right and the house is showcased properly." The reassurances did not cease at one reply. I further elaborated, "I will publish full page ads in the most popular real estate magazines. I will hold open houses every weekend until it sells." I tight roped the issue by promising effort, not results.

However, the industry leading agents, known as the sharks, simply understood the psychology of the client and shamelessly told clients exactly what they wanted to hear. "Yes, it will sell. I will sell it. Be rest assured it will sell." Regardless of the market conditions. The sharks knew that it was almost impossible for a house not to sell eventually. So, they made the claim without any fear of failing. If they did fail, and the house remained on the market for the duration of the listing agreement of 90 days, they packed up their For Sale sign and left as a different agent from a different brokerage came to take over the listing.

I felt inhibited from making unjustifiable promises. But the sharks made a good living off the puffery. They sold the excitement, the "sizzle" and the absolute "assuredness." I simply listened to the customers' and clients' desired attributes and found a match in the marketplace. If my customers were looking for a home in a particular neighborhood and wanted a brick façade, a sunroom, and finished walk out basement, I found it for them. If they were looking for a colonial with a Dutch roof, or a

100-year-old fixer-upper, I combed through the available listings and found the match.

Life Lesson 26: Success in sales can be accomplished by pandering to the client or relying on integrity. Both approaches work but relying on one's integrity is more rewarding.

5 Elaine

As I placed Edward and Carol's home on the market, hoping it would sell, I received a call from a woman in Texas, which was already hit hard by the oncoming national recession. At age 38, Elaine was a divorcé several times over and had a 16-year-old daughter. They were both beautiful and appeared like older and younger sisters. Elaine visited the Washington Metropolitan region for just a few days to go on interviews for a new job. The Texan economy was distressed, and people were moving from there to anywhere they could find good jobs. In Elaine's case, she was an administrative wizard and was interviewing for a job at the Department of Energy in the Weapons Department. The job required a top-secret clearance. She would have an executive position if selected, yet she stood only 5'2".

She was a striking woman with ample bosoms and a magnetic smile. She ran five to ten miles a day and was completely single. When she arrived at my office, I was immediately smitten and may have come across a little unctuous. After the initial prequalifying procedures, and asking her what kind of home she was interested in, I conducted my research.

All during the weekend she was in town, I chauffeured her to numerous homes on my researched list. I led her to all kinds of variations of homes in her price range and desired set of amenities. Our rapport was anchored in me pontificating about the amenities, city traffic patterns, interest rates, and other intellectualized content, until even I became bored with hearing myself. Then Elaine starting talking about Texas and her abusive former husband. The conversation suddenly transitioned into the personal world. She felt perfectly at ease opening up to a 23-year-old young man, 15 years her junior.

We found one townhome that was near where her job would likely be. It was actually perfect for her. A three-level townhome was pristine and was on a cul-de-sac, White Saddle Drive. The home had a large kitchen and spacious living room, vaulted bedroom ceilings. The view from the back door was of nothing other than the campus of the Department of Energy, where she would probably secure a job. But she had to think about it.

Around dinner time, we agreed to suspend our day's work and stopped at a rib barbecue restaurant to dine out. On our way in. Marylyn, one of the other agents from my office, happened to be seated with her family as I walked past with Elaine. She looked up and down at Elaine and then at me with a smirk. "Hot date tonight, Roy?"

I was taken back remembering the lengthy office meetings and repetitive emphasis on conducting ethical behavior. But was this an ethical dilemma? I dismissed the implied complications and simply replied, "No, I am just with a customer taking a break from looking at homes."

Marylyn's husband leaned over to her and whispered, "I wonder where he's looking for that house." They snickered thinking erotic thoughts. But I knew the unspoken rules about getting involved with customers and clients. It was considered unethical. I felt innocent however, and proceeded, until music came over the loudspeakers and Elaine grabbed my arm drawing me to the dance floor. I obliged her knowing this would certainly be misinterpreted by management. But still, we were just innocently dancing.

As the evening came to a close, Elaine said, "The next time I'm in town, I'll call you to see more houses." I drove her to her hotel and parted ways as I've done with many previous customers.

A few weeks later, Elaine did call. Only this time, she had been granted the job at the Department of Energy and would like to place a contract on the home I had shown her near there on White Saddle Drive. She could walk to work if she desired. All she needed now was to sign the paperwork. Elaine stayed at a hotel on sixth street in downtown Washington, DC. Over the phone, I said, "I can make it there in an hour with the paperwork."

I entered the hotel wearing my tie and suit with the contract at my side in my briefcase. At her door, I knocked. She let me in with a smile and after a brief exchange of niceties I presented her with the sales contract. She signed it confidently. And within minutes, my purpose for coming out in the dark evening to the big city was over. All that was left was to leave. That didn't happen. We looked into each other's eyes and melded into a tight hug. Business was done and we were both hungry for dinner. We decided to go and find some place that was open and experience the Washington food scene. We were near the famous Chinatown and came across an open restaurant where we shared a noodle dish as we walked the streets.

Elaine bubbled with excitement being a guest in the most powerful city in the world. The nightlife awakened our senses, as people and cars went in all directions before us, creating a lively and noisy ambience. We walked hand in hand for blocks with the only light coming from business signs and streetlights. We walked until we didn't know where we were, when stopped, hugged again, and kissed. She thrust her tongue into my mouth and caressed the inside. With the sensation driving me crazy, I held her tighter.

I never left her side that night and, in the morning, woke up next to her. My golden sports coat, representing the gold standard of my agency, lay on the floor as if it were the chalked outline of a dead man. My once carefully knotted tie lay unraveled in the shape of a snake. My formerly starched white shirt lay rumpled at the edge of the bed where I threw it after tearing it off in the heat of passion hours in the past. My pants were removed with such haste they were inside out. My pair of socks were nowhere near each other, and my underpants and belt were strewn elsewhere in the room, making it appear as if I swallowed a bomb that blew off my clothes and disintegrated my form.

Elaine had an appointment to meet the hiring representative from the Department of Energy at the hotel restaurant. Surprisingly, on several levels, Elaine invited me to join her for breakfast with this hiring rep. She apparently accepted my presence as her boyfriend.

After we parted, Elaine went to the airport to catch her flight back to Texas. I told her, "I'll let you know what happens with your offer on the house." Still wearing the previous day's clothes, I went home and showered before returning to the real estate office. At the office, I contacted the listing agent and indicated that I had a contract to present.

I felt fine, ethically speaking, sleeping with a customer. Afterall, that happened after the contact was signed. It was not as if there was a quid pro quo. Our passion that night began with a mutual hug and then on our walk the 38-year-old thrust her tongue into my mouth. I was obviously in the clear. We even had gone out to dinner and danced. She was my "girlfriend." Can't a real estate agent sell a home to someone they know, someone they have been intimate with? So why was this hanging over my head like a guillotine blade?

That night, I submitted my contract to the listing agent, Penelope Brubaker, and homeowners. Penelope was a striking divorcé, well into her forties. Her jet-black hair was cut evenly across her brows and the sides hung, curved to her ears. Her pale skin contrasted with a sharp, deep red lipstick. Penelope was a highly experienced multi-million dollar agent and, like a fearless shrew, bullied her clients and me. She snatched the contract out of my hands and immediately crossed out the bid price which fell shy of the listing price and announced in a way that sounded like a shriek, "This is not a full price offer. This is unacceptable." She had not consulted her clients who seemed to relinquish all critical thinking to their representative and cower in her presence.

"Everybody negotiates a little. That's normal," I protested knowing how much work it took to find a ready, willing, and able buyer and have them sign on the dotted line.

"Remember who you work for, Roy. You work for the sellers," Penelope admonished.

"I think I am working for the seller by bringing in a contract. They do want to sell their house, don't they?" I pleaded. The more resistance I brought up the greater Penelope's arrogance grew and dismissed me as if I were a waiter who brought his table the wrong food order.

"Go back to the buyer and bring me a full-priced contract," she scolded without a shred of fear that the buyer would back out altogether. I realized later that the agent probably wanted to keep the house on the market in the hopes that she could find a buyer herself and therefore, get a double commission for listing and selling the home.

The next day, I called Elaine and conveyed the seller's response to Elaine which greatly disappointed her. She was looking forward to moving in soon and using the den as a home office. As heartbreaking as it was to tell a customer to come up in price or look somewhere else, it was excruciating to tell a woman with whom I spent the night.

At the office, the office manager and the crew had another team meeting to cover the week's developments and any arising issues. Sometimes these meeting discussions turned into gossip parties of which agent was sleeping around and whose reputation drove them out of the industry. I squirmed in my seat upon hearing these stories. Though my guilty thoughts were always followed by comforting thoughts that I was truly taken with Elaine, and that there was nothing wrong with doing business with someone you love.

But beneath my own reassurances, I couldn't deny the optics and fact that I slept with the customer while representing the sellers. No matter how I skirted the issue, my mind was burdened by the dilemma.

During the meeting the office manager, Sherry, brought to our attention a contract prepared by Gertrude, a chain smoking, senior woman with a gravelly voice and wrinkled, leathery skin. She had a thick, German accent which didn't translate well over the phone, and she quickly gave up on cases that invited the first inkling of trouble. But trouble also seemed to follow her cases.

Sometimes it was her customers and clients who fueled the unrest, sometimes, as in this case, her own ineptitude was the causal factor in the great disruption that was sure to either lead to a lawsuit or a tarnishing of her reputation, which of course affects the office's reputation.

Gertrude in her role as agent between the customer and seller, wrote a contingency in the sales contract. Although no agent is a lawyer and needn't have any greater education than a six-week real estate course, we were expected to write legally binding contingencies. Gertrude wrote, *Buyer and seller agree that a six-foot fence be installed in a workman-like manner around the perimeter of the property known as 12 Vince Street at seller's expense prior to settlement.*

That verbiage was good enough for the settlement attorneys to accept as a valid contingency, except soon after the contract was signed by both parties, who were contentious with each other due to difficult negotiations, someone realized that the contingency, written by Gertrude, indicated the six-foot fence by using the abbreviated line marker instead of the word "foot" written out. That in itself wasn't the problem. If that was all there was, the contingency would still have been valid. But Gertrude used double lines, which indicates inches instead of the single line that indicates feet. So, in her eternal negligence, Gertrude required the seller to install a six "inch" fence around the perimeter of the property. The sellers had a field day laughing at the loophole worth thousands of dollars. One too many little lines besmirched the office's reputation. The broker was furious, and was ready to fire her and anyone else for the slightest infractions, whether they be technical errors or ethical breaches.

6   Primadona's Get Their Way

The first week into the month, the office chalkboard that tallied the monthly sales was eerily blank. After every sales contract became ratified from the office agents, Sherry, the office manager, proudly wrote the street name and value of each house sold with the responsible agent's name on the board. This was done not only to record the monthly sales but to also spur on the agents to hustle more. For many unproductive agents, however, the list was a sore spot and source of envy. Every agent wanted their name on the board to show their success and tease the jealousies of the other agents. All the while, the agents who lacked sales felt compelled to hide their true feelings and feigned support as best they could muster.

By the second week into the month, Mr. Kent was visibly shaken by the blank, nameless chalkboard. He depended on the agents to generate at least a million dollars in real estate sales each month, which infused about $15,000 per month into his pockets. As impressive as that sounded, he owned the historic building valued in the millions and paid a steep mortgage. Mr. Kent's gentile nature could noticeably change into a burly, grumble as he complained out loud, "Is anybody working the phones? Let's get going and start closing some deals." The anxiety in his voice was also becoming clearer to the rest of us.

As the pressures for sales productivity grew daily, Sherry compulsively ate chips to stave off the anxiety of a crew that produced nothing. Her frustration led to fear for her job. That fear turned to anger and desperation as she verbally fenced with the agents. The bickering erupted into shouting matches. "Why are you just sitting there Gertrude?" Sherry chastised.

"I'm just smoking," the old lady groveled.

"Well, get on the horn and make some cold calls."

Then Gertrude tried to revive her self-esteem by recalling the success of yesteryear.

"I don't know why I don't have sales. When I was younger, I had no trouble. The sales just came to me easily." Gertrude then realized her cigarette had burned and half of it, an ash stick titled and fell onto her lap. She jumped a bit and brushed the ashes onto the carpet. Then took another slow burning drag before reluctantly picking up the phone for yet another cold call to generate highly improbable success.

The agents walked in and out of the office with soured, dejected demeanors, except me. Unbeknownst to anyone else, I had been working on several leads which were all in various states of near completion. The day finally came near the end of the month when all my contracts were ratified. My briefcase contained three contracts: a massive colonial valued about $600,000, which was contracted by the couple who worked at Rockwell Aeronautics. Of course, to buy this huge house, the sale was contingent on the sale of their old home, which I listed and obtained a contract for $300,000.

The buyers of this listing, the Calloways, however, had a contingency to sell two of their properties, their primary home on Midway Avenue and their investment property, a townhouse on White Saddle Drive, which was the one Elaine had sought and was dismissed. After I reported to Elaine the attitude of the listing agent and how dismissive she was, I reminded Elaine of how perfect the home was for her needs and what a seller's market meant. "Sellers have the upper hand in a hot market. There are more buyers than listings," I explained. Then continued to remind her of the proximity to her job and the fabulous quiet neighborhood and all of the attributes of the home.

"You're not just pulling my leg now arya, Roy? You know to get a larger commission?" Elaine said hesitantly.

"Elaine. Really. We're talking about a mere three-thousand-dollar difference. That amounts to about $45 more in commission for me. That's no incentive to trick you," I said balancing my emotions between being offended and reassuring her.

"Yeah, well, three thousand dollars is a lot to me," she tried to counter.

"Elaine," I started softly, "You will be amortizing that $3,000 over 30 years. It raises your monthly mortgage by no more than 21 dollars. Is that worth losing out on the perfect home?" I questioned rhetorically.

"I guess not." She acquiesced and agreed to come full price. Despite the new bid, the listing agent didn't like being preempted from finding her own buyer, but by law, she had to present the contract, which was ratified at a value of $136,000. The three sales, valued in excess of $1 million dollars, were interlocked through contingencies, which made for a very precarious state of affairs. Should the buyer at the beginning of the link fail to obtain their loan, the entire link would fall like a house of cards.

At least I had ratified contracts, which meant my name and properties got listed on the chalkboard. The tension in the office made the agents walk softly. I was in a bubble of my own, completely in mirth at my success while everyone else was cringing and walking as if they were no longer moving through air but enduring the resistance of water.

While my contracts were stacked in my briefcase, I watched Sherry get fatter by the moment as she tried to manage her anxieties by eating her way through a bag of chocolate covered popcorn. Lifting herself from her chair took a major effort when she felt it necessary to come into the crew room. She wore a dress which, like a parachute, blanketed her massive rotund girth. Only her enormous calves and Flintstone ankles were revealed as she puttered around as the office mother hen. After she pecked on one of the agents with some critical remark about their zero production, I waited until the behemoth woman returned to her desk. When I heard the sound of her heft sink into the cushion of the chair, I called her, "Oh Sherry?" A bit perturbed that I asked her to come out to the crew room from where she had just come, she looked at me hopefully. I snapped open my briefcase and pulled out a manilla folder containing my smallest ratified contract, a $136,000 townhouse. Sherry's face lit up from furrowed to the world's happiest person. It was like Christmas morning, I gave her the contract, and she hustled to the chalkboard and wrote the street address, sales value, and my name. Even though it was a small contract, it broke the month's curse of non-productivity. She came back in the crew room and chastised the other agents, "You all need to get off your duffs and close some deals." Then to rub it in, she said, "like Roy."

Marylyn smiled and reassured Sherry, "I'm working with clients to get a listing for a colonial south of Rt. 28." Sherry snapped back, "Don't talk to me about possibilities. You should be closing sales, we have nearly zero listings. That's not acceptable." Then again, she jabbed the agents with toxic words designed to evoke optimal embarrassment by interjecting my name. "If Roy, who's only been with us for a year and a half, can bring in a contract, you all certainly can."

Then Fran and Lilly growled back, "The economy is tanking, Sherry. People are taking their time these days. But things will turn around. We have some clients who want to list their land. The only issue is that there is a sink hole on the property. And it's getting larger and they don't want to pay for taking care of it. But we're working on it."

Sherry looked up to the heavens, silently asking why these two ladies always have to have complicated transactions. Then Chuck came in to the office wearing cut off shorts which were stained with motor oil. "Where do you think you are?" Sherry blasted him.

"Oh, I've got some customers to show some homes," he said nonchalantly.

"Well, that's great but are you selling them a garage? She asked sarcastically.

Chuck looked puzzled and clueless to his appearance. "Wear your golden jacket and proper attire Chuck," Sherry rightfully castigated. Then she said, "Roy just got a sale."

Chuck spied the chalkboard and made a face of dismissiveness then rationalized, "That's a little sale." He recomposed himself and said, "I mean great job Roy. But I'm working on a really huge deal."

I smiled back to acknowledge him. I waited for Sherry to lumber back to her office. With each of her heavy steps, the office windows shook. I listened carefully for the sound of the percussion as she collapsed her buttocks onto the desk chair. Then I sang out her name, "Oh, Sherry?"

Not wanting to exert herself again getting up, she replied, "What?"

"Can you come here a moment?" I asked.

She reluctantly stood up and shook the windows with each heavy step until entering the crew room. The other agents were getting anxious as they watched the scene unfold. "What is it?" Sherry asked pointedly. I snapped open my briefcase, pulled out another manilla folder and handed it to her. She opened it up and her beaming face told the story. "Another contract," She nearly yelped. This time, the other agents appeared confused. They didn't know how to react.

They just gave their disingenuous support a moment ago. Sherry nearly sashayed to the chalkboard and wrote, Timely Square, $300,000, Roy. And proudly walked back, congratulated me, and sneered at the other agents who tried to disguise their envy.

Gertrude stubbed out her cigarette and lit another one, sucked in a deep breath, blew out the smoke and nervously tapped the end of ash into the trash bin.

I watched Sherry turn and walk back to her desk. Just as I heard her seat compress, I called, "Oh, Sherry," I could hear her spring out of the chair, the windows shook as she heavily stepped into the crew room wide eyed and incredulous but hoping for just one more miracle. I snapped open my briefcase again and handed her another manilla folder. She opened it up and I thought she was going to fall to the ground as hard as King Kong fell from the Empire State Building. She then found her way to the chalkboard and wrote Green Hill Road, $600,000, Roy.

The other agents were suppressing their exasperation as best they could. How can eleven agents produce zero sales while I, still considered a punk rookie, generate nearly a million dollars in real estate sales in just one month. Some agents showed their sorrows with visible consternation. They hung their heads. They cleared their throats, trying to comprehend this canyon of disparity.

I, on the other hand, had no other contracts to tease the office manager with. Though I was tempted to sing out her name one more time just to see her jump out of her chair a fourth time only for me to ask her to get me a cup of water, but I thought that to be too cruel. She may get a heart attack. So, I smiled at her and started research on the multiple listing service to find the perfect home….for myself.

***

I was a true believer in the value of real estate ownership. So much so that I wanted one for myself. I searched the multiple listing service high and low for something that I could afford. I found a townhouse, which were averaging more than $100,000, a 40 percent increase in a year and a half. I went to the site where the listing was, which happened to be a new housing development and the townhouse in question was under construction. I walked on the property and cautiously through the skeletal two-by-fours seeing the embryonic rooms without walls and staircases without railings. I walked across the particle-board floors to the back of the house and saw the most spectacular view of the community lake. The ripples of the water's surface reflected the sunshine like the glint in an eye one thousand times over.

I checked the MLS listing that indicated all the features of the house and other notes such as the $7,000 extra fee for the lot location, which backed up to the lake. As outrageous as that charge was, few homes backed up to a thin forest that accented a mile long, glistening lake. I found my home.

I placed a contract on it immediately.

***

Before I could reach my own settlement of my newfound home, I had to see my three sales contracts through to their settlements.

My sale of the McMansion to the technocratic power couple was contingent on the sale of their current split-level home. Within weeks, a Southern couple, Buddy and Blanche Calloway, placed an offer on the technocrats' split-level house with a contingency that they sell their old, small, Cape Cod with a listing price of $115,000. I happened to have customers looking in that price range.

I first came into contact with Abayomrunkoje and Ababuo Agwuegbo from a call into the office. They had migrated from Nigeria a year ago and were renting an apartment in Washington, DC, but felt they were ready to lay their roots into home ownership as permanent residents of the Metropolitan region.

After I prequalified them, I agreed that they were financially qualified candidates for home ownership and that they would benefit greatly from tax deductions and a fixed mortgage. As usual, Abayomrunkoje and Ababuo were very different from me. They were older and married, looking for a home.

I felt, here we go again, I have to try to establish rapport with people I have nothing in common. But a surprising thing happened, Abayomrunkoje asked me, "So young man, are you married? What is your situation? Do you own a house too?" So, it wasn't long before I shared my relatively short biographical history with them. But this time I enthusiastically told them how eager I was to buy my own home. Ababuo reassured me, "We've all been there…at the beginning. It's hard to get established." They could relate to my youth having been there before and encouraged me to pursue my dream for an independent life, "You're on the right path, my friend."

Life Lesson 31: Establishing rapport becomes easier with maturity, life experiences, and common interests.

The outings were always easy going as we all talked about the houses and more candid matters. I listened intently as they spoke about their early years living in Nigeria and how different everything here was. And they appreciated my attentive ear.

As the weeks passed, I showed them dozens of homes of all sorts. But I never got inpatient. They believed in me and I in them. They said that I was showing them fine homes and that they just had to choose the best one for themselves. Ababuo disclosed, "We have seen many homes with two other real estate agents before calling you Roy, and they were both too pushy." Ababuo complained, "One of the other agents kept showing us houses that were so much money. So high. Way above our comfort zone. And the other only showed us her own listings."

I admitted "Many agents want to sell their own listings or the highest priced homes for sake of a larger commission. But I assure you I will only show you homes that meet your interests."

After I showed Abayomrunkoje and Ababuo the Midway Avenue home, they beamed with delight at all of the amenities, the large eat-in kitchen, the spacious back yard, the proximity to Washington, DC and the main highway. Ababuo said, "It reminds me of my grandmother's home where I played as a little girl." Abayomrunkoje and Ababuo were so excited about the Midway home, I drove them to my office where they happily signed a full-priced sales contract.

Life Lesson 32: An agent can sell a greater volume of homes if he/she simply finds homes that match the wishes of the home buyer, instead of trying to push them into something they can't afford.

Now I just had to get them to settlement so that the sellers would be able to settle on my listing, which would enable my technocratic clients to settle on their new home. All of my contracts were linked with each other like a line of dominoes that if any part should fall, the remaining parts would fall too. I would either see three settlements with three commissions totaling $17,000 or nothing.

The marketplace was getting jumpy, stricken with an approaching panic of a national recession. Small time agents were quitting. Homeowners were delaying their decisions to put their homes up for sale. Worse yet thousands of people were getting laid-off from work, making them unqualified to obtain a loan. And those still looking, were increasingly failing to qualify for a loan because of rising interest rates.

Businesses across the land were closing. And like a virus, the closure of one business led to another, then another. The loss of jobs accelerated, hitting all industries, especially the real estate market.

Even my contract for the home I was purchasing was contingent on me securing a mortgage loan, which would be approved if I came up with another $17,000, the amount of commissions for my next three sales. They all would finalize on the same settlement date.

As I walked toward an apartment building to pick up a customer, I witnessed an astonishing and frightening omen. I saw one of my fellow heavy-hitting real estate agents from another agency outside the complex wearing an orange uniform with a silly fast-food paper hat. She was holding a pizza box making a delivery. When our eyes locked, she simply said, withholding the embarrassment, "I'm making a little extra money on the side. My mortgage is a lot." I understood precisely, in that getting one's commission check could take months from first introducing oneself to a customer to when the customer signs the last page of a large stack of settlement papers. But seeing this former titan of sales wearing an orange costume and matching colored Pizza-Go cap, she looked ridiculous, juvenile, and shamed into submission.

Meanwhile at the office, the young kid, Bryce, who followed me into the sales staff as a newbie, finally called it quits after two years and only one sale, which was to his mother, who bought a small townhouse. I don't know what happened to him, but Sherry told me that he saw me making all of these sales, one after another, and he just got discouraged.

As I rose to become the top producing agent in the office, the sales crew thinned out with some retiring, some moving away, others quitting out of frustration. But Mr. Kent never fired anyone, especially for a lack of productivity. Little expense was required to keep an agent onboard. A broker always hoped an agent will one day learn the trade and be productive. Even the young one, Bryce, who quit, was able to sell a house to his mother. This paltry sales performance was what many new agents experienced. They get into the business and buy their own house or sell their family house, only to never convert an actual customer into a buyer.

Damage to a broker's reputation due to a lawsuit or breach of ethics was cause for dismissal. And as it turned out, Elaine wasn't in love with me as I thought. She had resented having to come up in price and believed I was squeezing her out of more money for the sake of the seller and for a larger commission. After her deal went to settlement, our relationship dissolved into nothing but a bitter threat that she would complain of my boorish and exploitive behavior to the office manager, Sherry.

Although I was certain that if the worst-case scenario occurred, and I did indeed get fired for my physical involvement with Elaine, I was confident I could get a real estate sales job with another broker fairly easily. They weren't all so judgmental. However, this particular broker, Mr. Kent and Sherry were very old school. Very religious. And very keen on keeping a squeaky-clean image. My primary concern was getting fired before my other three linked sales went to settlement and losing out on earning the commissions. Was Elaine bluffing or was she out for blood?

I went to Elaine's newly purchased home and knocked on her door. She opened the door surprised to see me standing before her, "Well look who it is," she said. But she didn't slam the door on me, so I took that as a good sign.

"Hi," I finally uttered, still overtaken by her beauty.

"What are you doing here?" she asked.

"What do you mean? I miss you, Elaine. I wanted to know how you and your daughter are doing. You know, moving in, settling in. All that," I finally said.

She let me into the foyer, which was progress I believed. Elaine appeared sexy as always, and I was pleased to be in her presence again despite her earlier threat. My feelings for her seemed to erase the resentment I had been harboring since she settled on her home.

As the man in the relationship, I felt obligated to apologize to her. "Listen Elaine, I am sorry for whatever perceived issue there was between us." But the way I couched that apology seemed disingenuous to her, roiling her even more. How dare I apologize in a way that suggested there could be some other valid perception of my indecent and unethical behavior. And suddenly, I again was the villain. I was shooed out with the complementary slam of the door.

When I came back into the office, Sherry was there and I could feel her judgmental eye darting at me. Her look was one that I assumed knew all about my dalliances with Elaine, who must have called the office and complained about me. I thought the shit was about to hit the propellers, and I would have to take flight into the sunset of fired real estate agents.

***

I believed that Sherry and Mr. Kent knew all about Elaine. The scenario had scandal written all over it. And it threatened the promise of the biggest payday of my life: three consecutive settlements on one day worth not only $17,000 in commissions, but also what that money would enable me to buy for myself: my first home.

Although keeping together the link of three sales contracts was somewhat of a trick in itself, I didn't need the possibility of getting sacked as a distraction. But I started to obsess that management was preparing to do just that. Would they fire me and assume control over my sales and keep my part of the commission for themselves? That could tempt anyone with a streak of dishonesty. That would be ironic if they were motivated by financial greed to fire me for my questionable ethical actions.

I couldn't help but examine the issue from all points of view. What if I besmirched the office's reputation, who would actually know or even care that an agent fooled around with a customer? It was not as if it was a featured story televised on the national news. And if they did fire me, they would lose all of the potential income that I could be bringing in. Heck, I was the top producing agent. If they canned me, they may gain my most immediate commissions, but not the promise of future wealth. I found this situation ironic as well in that by cutting me out, they would be cutting into their own livelihood. I was umbilically connected by shared commissions with them.

More importantly, I examined the issue introspectively. Did I truly jeopardize the broker's reputation through unethical behavior? I had studied ethics in many college classes. And in those studies, ethics always pertained to acting in a way that was determined prohibited; not as a law or right, but as a relative red line that shouldn't be crossed. By doing so, one's unethical behavior harms or exploits someone else. I couldn't conceive that my dalliance would cause anybody harm. It was a private matter between Elaine and me.

Frankly, it was no one else's business. Perhaps, I thought, management's objection is unethical towards Elaine and me—an encroachment on our privacy and right. Who, other than those intimately involved, should care who engages with whom? Based on religious doctrine or prudish standards, there was violation; but in relation to late 20th century behavior, it's passé, irrelevant, and unsurprising. I thought of my own interests. I fell for Elaine. As it turned out, she ultimately soured on me. But that was her choice based on her perceptions. And it was her choice to vocalize the matter to management. Where are the ethics in relation to that encroachment on my reputation and the impact on my future with the company?

Life Lesson 33: ethics can be relative to the eye of the beholder and the premise by which it is founded.

I took note of my own behavior and tried to convince myself that I did wait until after Elaine signed the contract before getting intimate with her. But with each refute of the facts, I felt as if the optics always won. My relationship muddled the waters in which I was now drowning. It was a textbook case of dipping one's pen in the company ink.

Any which way I turned the tables, I sounded as if I was rationalizing the obvious caveat: don't mix business with pleasure. This became my textbook folly. But I couldn't undo the past and now the issue was how do I deal with the fall out?

As the weeks passed, nothing changed other than Sherry's evil eye impaling me when we passed each other in the office. And the occasional office announcements about upholding our high ethical standards, which was brought up as an unnerving slight against me. But no firing.

Every Wednesday, the office was full of the agents for the weekly staff meeting. Sherry sat in a chair as at the helm to cover the issues of the day. She discussed industry news, sales performance of the crew, and routine matters about contracts. But she always personalized the meetings with interjections of her own past experiences. As a staple to her real estate sermons, Sherry preached about ethics, "You want to always remember the Golden Rule," she would start off. "Always treat others the way you would want to be treated." This point was surely icing over a hot mess of manipulative treachery in the arsenal of salesmanship. If anything, agents didn't treat customers the way we would want to be treated. The veteran sales agents did everything they could to push around, bully, manipulate, and close their clients and customers. It was the art of controlling human behavior.

But I had no issue with what she was saying. I did treat my customers as I would want to be treated. I was fair, informative and polite. I actually believed in the product I was selling. As far as I was concerned, I felt good about my relationships with my customers. Although, I felt Sherry was singling me out and shaming me through verbal code, telling me I breached the ethical red line. Despite Sherry's occasional darting glare that reached into my retinas and innuendos during the meetings, I felt at peace with all that had transpired. But I was continually reminded that whether I could live with myself or not had nothing to do with getting fired. My destiny was more in the hands of management.

Sherry then blended her uncanny ability to impart information by means of gossiping. She brought up a former real estate agent, who, engaged in affairs with her male customers. "She developed a reputation that stained her broker's good name." Then Sherry, with no compunction, stated the agent's name as if to brand her before us all. "Her name was Delores Windmeir and she was kicked out of her broker's crew and no one wanted to hire her." I was certain she was about to use such symbolic words as "Banished," and "Ostracized." But she used her own means of wordsmithing. She would repeat the agent by her full name, "Delores Windmeir was forced out the real estate industry altogether." She concluded at this climatic precipice to instill a primal fear as she then smiled and encouraged us to close deals.

In the end, all the talk about ethics and competence that was emphasized in every staff meeting, the "pious" broker and critical manager never once took action against any agent, including me, for any reason. Sherry was content with just hanging the issue over my head as a suggested threat. Ultimately, what mattered to them all was that we agents brought money into the office.

Life Lesson 34: The almighty dollar trumped ethical infractions.

Somehow, I felt I needed to realize my fortune in sales before I met the fate of Delores Windmeir. The day of my settlements was fast approaching. Did I play with Sherry's emotions too much? Was she going to pre-empt my settlements with a last-minute execution? Perhaps, I had become too big too fast, a lion among kittens. Maybe, I was embarrassing the other agents into submission. Sherry may believe, the rest of the agents would perform better if I wasn't around. I didn't know what to think, which was an odd feeling because I was used to my own confidence. But this situation was different. My future could be derailed by Mr. Kent or Sherry on an emotional whim.

7   Settlement

The day of my settlements: I met my customers, Ababuo and Abayomrunkoje at the settlement office. Awaiting us were the attorney, who reclined while sucking on some breath mints, and a senior-aged Caucasian couple, originally from Mississippi and whiter than a Klansman's robe. The tension in the room seemed instant as we walked in and the sellers took a gander of the charcoal-skinned customers who were buying their home. An unspoken contempt was flogging us before a word was exchanged.

Upon seeing my customers, the white couple, Buddy and Blanche Conolly, seemed beside themselves. They glanced at each other, then Buddy touched his wife's fingers as a way to reassure her and maintain their composure. They were thinking that they very well may go to Hell if their former neighbors knew who would be moving into their Midway Avenue home.

The attorney, still sucking his mints, placed a stack of papers on the settlement table, and introduced himself to begin the settlement. Buddy looked at the stack of papers and saw an opportunity to voice how perturbed he and Blanche were. "We gotta sign all these papers?" he asked in a bellicose manner causing a quake in the room that unsettled everyone. The attorney reassured everyone that all the papers were in order and necessary to sign.

Both Buddy and Abayomrunkoje peered at each document while inwardly scheming how to weasel out of the obligation. They were both reluctant to sign necessary papers. Ababuo and Abayomrunkoje felt uneasy, disrespected by Buddy and Blanche's unprovoked anger. Buying a home was a bold move for anyone. The house was usually one of the largest investments of one's life. The mortgage may take a 30-year commitment to pay off. Most buyers faced this daunting challenge with a great deal of anxiety and uncertainty. Customers often experienced "buyer's remorse," a riptide that pulls them emotionally in the opposite direction from embracing their purchase. All these feelings were just beneath the calm exterior. And not much was needed to tip the balance of civility to reveal the raw feelings of prejudice, buyer's remorse, anxiety, and uncertainty. The collapse of settlement was just one slight away.

Then the customer's complaint from the walkthrough emerged. Abayomrunkoje spoke up, "During the walkthrough, the doorbell and a light...they did not work." Buddy nearly lost it, thinking how dare they now try to blame them for having a faulty home. The attorney interjected, "Issues resulting from the walkthrough are usually negotiated so the settlement can continue to completion. How's about the sellers set aside the sum of $500 in escrow until the doorbell issue is resolved?" This was a routine solution, but this time, Abayomrunkoje and Ababuo raised the possibility that it was not just the doorbell that didn't function. The light in the hallway also failed to turn on. "There could be a whole electrical wiring problem," Abayomrunkoje complained. "We think $5,000 should be set in escrow."

Buddy nearly fell off his seat, but managed to remain seated and yelled back, "I'm not putting anything into escrow, damn it. Take it or leave it," he said feeling that if Ababuo and Abayomrunkoje didn't want to buy their house as is, good riddance.

The buyers would not be bullied. Both parties couldn't agree on how much the seller should place in escrow. The sellers bitterly agreed to a symbolic $100 believing the doorbell and hall light failures were isolated issues. The buyers were skeptical and equally mistrusting and would not be persuaded. With this stalemate, the buyers looked at each other, stood up, and walked out. The attorney announced, "There is no settlement."

My jaw dropped as I gawked at the sellers and the settlement attorney wishing for a different outcome. My dream of purchasing my own home depended on this settlement so that the following two settlements later that day could also take place. Maybe the settlement attorney and sellers could suck it up for another four months and start the process all over with another buyer, but I couldn't. And, I was unwilling to let this go lightly. I stood up and hurried after the buyers. They had already reached the parking lot. I ran across the lot calling out to them in desperation. Catching up to them, and out of breath, I asked them, "Is this what you really want?" I reminded them how quaint and cozy the Cape Cod felt and how affordable it was. I told them the prices of all homes had already increased some 10 percent since they signed for this one. "It's like you're getting paid $10,000 to move in," I reasoned. Feeling I was getting too factual with abstract numbers and heady concepts, I finally realized the power in the relationship was the woman and that I needed to appeal to her sensibilities. "And that large kitchen you always wanted. It's the perfect starter home to begin a family. You will enjoy it just like you did as a little girl. You aren't going to let those people deny you your right for a piece of the American dream, are you?" I don't know where my awareness of the triggers came from, certainly not from any textbook, but I found the way to win them over.

Life Lesson 35: Persuasion entails appealing to people's deepest self-interests.

Ababuo and Abayomrunkoje took a moment to discuss the matter in an exchange of whispers. Then an extraordinary thing happened. They actually turned around and returned to the settlement office where they signed all the papers.

We all went to the house again to resolve the outstanding issues. If it turned out to be a major electrical problem, I would contact an electrician to remedy the electrical system and it would be paid by the sellers per the terms of the original contract.

It turned out the light that didn't illuminate was connected to a wall switch that just needed to be flipped on, and the doorbell just needed replacement. No catastrophe, except the one averted.

I returned to the office emotionally spent and relieved that my sale remained listed on the office chalkboard:

Sale:

Roy C. Luschman, Midway Ave., $115,000. 10/15/1988

Settled Commission: $1,720

Life Lesson 36: Sometimes you possess the power to control an out-of-control situation.

At the moment the buyers signed the last document to complete the settlement, I realized how focused I was in the present and how I reveled in my profession of last choice. The anxieties and depression of trying to complete a 20-page report on time for a class during college was replaced by the exhilaration of completing a transaction and marching it to settlement. I realized I was no longer a depressed student trying to earn a grade so that employers could predict whether I could do their job. I now had experience which was evidence that I can do the job. I realized every poor grade I ever received was no longer relevant. They did not define my life.

My productivity in real estate resulted from my pursuits, understanding of customer's interests, and sales psychology. The intangibles such as establishing rapport, persuasion, and handling objections were never taught through any textbook. Equally as true was that I no longer answered hypothetical questions, such as "Should you obey an unjust law?" Faced with such real ethical dilemmas, I was forced to make my decisions and live with the results. I was no longer a student wondering what to do with my life. I was living it with a growing sales volume that confirmed my self-worth.

Life Lesson 37: Being true to your own integrity is the best ethical standard.

As the day continued, I successfully completed the following two settlements and readied myself for the settlement of my own home.

Life Lesson 38: Entering the real world relies more than textbook knowledge. Intangible qualities such as effort, persistence, and honesty can take you far into the world you make for yourself.

Sherry, with a heart full of acerbic feelings toward me, grew up shaped by social morés of yesteryear and a strictness that guilted her every thought about such ordinary human behavior as intimacy. With her shaming sword, she tried to impale me, yet she walked to the chalkboard and forced herself to write "settled" after each of my sales for the month of October 1988. No other agents' names accompanied mine.

October Sales, 1988

Roy C. Luschman, Midway Avenue, $115,000, 10/15/1988
- Settled Commission: $1,720

Roy C. Luschman, Timely Square, $300,000, 10/15/1988
- Settled Commission: $4,500

Roy C. Luschman, Green Hill Road, $600,000, 10/15/1988
- Settled Commission: $9,000

Roy C. Luschman, Island View Circle, $115,000, 10/25/1988
- Settled Commission: $1,720

Later that year, the National Real Estate Association awarded me a plaque for settling more than $2 million in sales for the year. My business cards were reprinted to read "Roy C.

Luschman A Multi-Million Dollar Agent." I may not have been considered "rich" at that point, but I generated more than a million in sales that October and hauled in about $17,000 in commissions. I even earned a commission for buying my own home, which I entered with my key and slept in for the first time, dreaming bigger stuff to come. Perhaps I should run for public office.

Textbook Follies follows the life of recent college graduate Roy C. Luschman from throwing his graduation cap into the air to throwing himself into the real world. The only problem is that despite reading about 75 textbooks while a student, Roy knows little about real life or what to do with the rest of his life. Facing the question "How does one get a first job, if it requires having had past work experience?" Roy sets out to answer that predicament and is astonished at his assent in a cut-throat industry.